Layla   Jayden   Caleb

They are Kid Force 3.

8

"Mrs Fox does love cookies," said Layla.

"Why did she jump out of the window?" asked Jayden.

"Maybe she's really, really hungry," said Layla.

"Wait! Look at these cookies," said Caleb.

12

"Wow! What happened to Mrs Fox?" asked Layla.

"The toxic cookies are making her grow. That's why she needs to keep eating," said Caleb.

"When will she stop?" asked Jayden.

"She won't," replied Caleb.

"I can build a machine. It will change her back," said Caleb.

"We can help," said Layla and Jayden.

"We will need a lot of energy," said Caleb.

"I can supply that," replied Jayden.

"And a lot of cookies," added Caleb.

"I can get those," replied Layla.

At the cookie factory...

Come on, Mrs Fox.

Here are some more cookies!

Don't snatch! It's rude.

25

28